The Mystery of
One Wish Pond

Suddenly a scream split the air, followed by a loud crack and a swooshing noise. Both boys scrambled from their sleeping-bags and fumbled in the dark for their jackets.

Chills raced up Beka's spine. "Good job, Rob. You scared *me* that time."

Robbie touched her shoulder.

Flinching, she twirled to face him. "How'd you get behind me? I thought you were over there." She flung her arm in the direction of the noise.

Before he could answer, she continued, "I think it's time to stop making spooky noises. I'm starting to feel sorry for these guys."

Robbie's face looked as pale as the boys'.

"Rob, what's wrong?"

"I didn't ma⬚⬚⬚⬚⬚⬚⬚," he stammered. "I-I thought y⬚⬚

Also in the Ghost Twins series

Have you read?
The Mystery at Kickingbird Lake

Look out for:
The Mystery on Walrus Mountain
The Missing Moose Mystery

Ghost Twins

2

The Mystery of One Wish Pond

Dian Curtis Regan

Hippo

*For David Curtis and Donna Curtis Sivesind,
with fond memories of camping trips and scary
noises in the night*

Scholastic Children's Books,
7-9 Pratt Street, London NW1 0AE, UK
a division of Scholastic Publications Ltd
London ~ New York ~ Toronto ~ Sydney ~ Auckland

First published in the US by Scholastic Inc., 1994
Published in the UK by Scholastic Publications Ltd, 1995

Copyright © Dian Curtis Regan, 1994

ISBN 0 590 13322 5

Typeset by TW Typesetting, Midsomer Norton, Avon
Printed by Cox & Wyman Ltd, Reading, Berks.

10 9 8 7 6 5 4 3 2 1

JUNIPER DAILY NEWS

New Autumn Fashions Inside!

Today's Highlights

Twins Involved in Boating Mishap

Robert Adam Zuffel and his twin sister, Rebeka Allison, seem to be victims of a boating accident at Kickingbird Lake. Their dog, Thatch, disappeared with them. Family members say that the twins had gone hiking on Mystery Island and were probably returning when yesterday's windstorm blew up.

Their overturned canoe was floating in the water off Mystery Island. A party of family members searched the lake and the surrounding area, and no trace of the twins or their dog was found.

President Roosevelt Welcomes Cary Grant to White House   pg.2

Zoot Suits All the Rage   pg.3

Movie Review: *Bambi*   pg.5

Local Student Wins Award for Model of All 48 States   pg.6

Contents

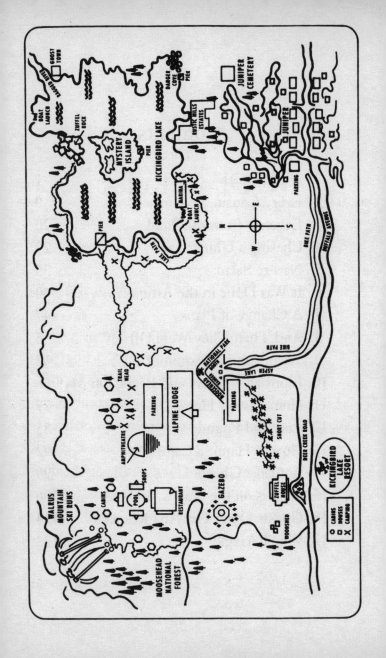

Chapter 1
Ghost Rules

Beka Zuffel eyed the triple-decker ice-cream cone.

Butter pecan. Her favourite flavour.

If only the teenage lifeguard sitting in a deck chair next to Kickingbird Lake Resort's swimming pool would put the cone down, she'd help herself to a couple of quick licks.

Nobody puts an ice-cream cone down, Beka's mind told her. And as long as the guy held on to it, she couldn't touch it. Her hand would swish right through his, cone and all – ghost rule number one.

Splash!

Beka tore her eyes from the butter pecan

1

cone. Splashes and shouts had filled the air all afternoon on this unusually warm autumn day.

But that last splash and shout were different.

Thatch, her dog, had done the splashing. And Robbie, her twin brother, was doing the shouting.

What had happened? Beka hurried to the edge of the pool. Across the way, Robbie was on his knees, trying to coax Thatch out of the water.

The dog was frantically trying to "save" a young girl whose sister was tossing her into the air, then letting her splash under. In a few seconds, the girl would surface, laughing.

"It's OK, boy!" Robbie yelled. "They're just playing a game."

"Poor Thatch." Beka circled the pool, wondering if the ghost dog understood why his paws went through the girl he was trying to save.

When she got to Robbie's side, she found him standing motionless, gaping at the water.

"What's wrong?"

"She didn't come up the last time." His voice sounded strained.

Beka watched. The older girl seemed puzzled; then panicked. She dived under, looking for her sister. In all the commotion, nobody noticed.

Even the lifeguard, who'd already gobbled all three scoops of ice-cream, was distracted, pulling a shirt on over his trunks.

Thatch became as frantic as the girl. His throaty *woofs* boomed across the water as he dog-paddled through the deep end – only no one could hear his barking or Beka's cries for help.

"We've got to do something!" Robbie yelped.

The sister, clinging to the side of the pool, shouted for help in such a tiny, scared voice that nobody heard.

Beka raced towards the lifeguard. "Look!" she shouted into his ear.

He straightened his shirt and smoothed his hair, then knelt to riffle though a canvas bag with ERIC embroidered on the side.

Even though people couldn't hear them, Beka knew they could "get someone's attention" – ghost rule number two. Was it a disturbance in the air? A direct message to the quietest corner of someone's mind?

She didn't know. But it worked.

Beka knelt next to the lifeguard and chanted: "Eric! Eric! Eric! Look at the pool! We need your help!"

In a flash, Eric leaped to his feet, almost as if Beka's words had burst though the barrier from her world to his.

"*Tweeeet!*" He blew his whistle, right in Beka's face.

She covered her ears. How could blowing a whistle be any help at all?

Eric ripped off the shirt he'd just put on and dived into the pool.

Thatch swam to meet the lifeguard, then led him to the girl. Of course, the lifeguard didn't *know* he was being led to the girl. By a ghost dog.

Voices around the pool hushed. A few urged the lifeguard on.

In seconds, Eric snatched the girl from under water and pulled her to safety.

Robbie helped Thatch climb from the pool, but couldn't hold on to him.

The dog wiggled his way *through* the bystanders to stand guard over the girl while Eric revived her.

Cheers filled the air when the girl sat up and began to cry.

Her ashen-faced sister hung back, clutching a deck chair and shivering. Water dripped from her wet bathing suit.

Beka wished she could hand the girl a towel, or comfort her in some way. But the girl would never know it.

Satisfied, Thatch bounded around the pool, jumping up on Beka for a hug. Even though he'd been in the water, his fur was completely dry. Ghost rule number three: rules of the world didn't apply to them.

"Good job, Thatch," Beka cooed to him. "You're my favourite puppy."

Robbie caught up with them and gave the dog's neck a good rubbing. "All in a day's work, huh, Thatch?"

A crisp wind kicked up. The "fun" shouts

turned shrill as swimmers pulled themselves from the pool and raced for towels. Fallen leaves from overhanging branches swirled into whirlwinds, making tourists fold lounge chairs and head for the lodge.

Eric turned the pool's OPEN sign to CLOSED. Then he found the girls' mother, and handed over her daughters, along with a few tips on pool safety.

"Time to go," Robbie said. "Think it's safe to return to the house?"

"The cleaners should be finished by now." Beka grasped Thatch's chain collar and led him through the narrow gate from the pool area. "We've stayed away all day to let them kick up as much dust as they pleased."

Thatch was the one bothered most when the cleaners came between guest families at the "old Zuffel house" – now that it was a holiday home at the Kickingbird Lake Resort. The dog would sneeze and sneeze until the twins took him outside.

Beka *liked* being in the house with the cleaners. It gave her a chance to practise her haunting skills. Like the time she kept dumping dry rags into a bucket of sudsy water. The cleaner finally gave up and used them for wet cleaning rags, so Beka started taking them *out* of the bucket and laying them flat to dry.

That was the day Robbie stayed busy downstairs unplugging the vacuum cleaner each time the worker got it going – ha!

The twins headed down Aspen Lane towards their house. Robbie played chase with Thatch. "Who do you think will move in next?" he asked.

"Certainly someone who will bother us." Beka sighed. Her brother liked strangers coming to stay in their house. She didn't. She'd rather have the place to herself, like they did the first fifty years, before Mr Tavolott bought the house and fixed it up as a holiday home.

As the twins neared the short cut, running from the main road through the sand plum grove to their own back garden, Thatch stopped, ears alert, one paw poised in mid-air.

"Aha!" Beka said. "He knows from this far away someone is invading our house again."

Ghost rule number four: Thatch's ghost powers were a mite stronger than theirs.

"Hey, boy!" Robbie called. "Are they friend or foe?"

Thatch began to yip and yowl at whatever signal he was picking up. Then he was off, disappearing through the trees.

Robbie raised his eyebrows. "What does *that* mean?"

"It must mean our new guests are waiting for us." Beka skipped ahead, laughing. "Let's give them a ghost greeting they'll never forget."

Chapter 2
Every Cousin for Himself

When the twins arrived at the house, they found the front door propped open with a jar of peanut butter.

The sight of an open door pleased Beka. *Closed* doors + ghosts = impossible task: ghost rule number five.

Two boys carried sleeping-bags inside and dumped them in the hall at the foot of the curved stairway. The boys were opposites: one, tall, blond, thin; the other, short and pudgy, with dark hair. Both seemed about eleven – the twins' age.

"Hey, Aunt Jenny!" the shorter boy called. "Can we eat lunch before we unpack?"

"Aunt Jenny?" Beka stepped outside. She hadn't noticed anyone else.

At the far end of the gravel drive stood a young woman dressed in jeans and hiking boots, talking to a man in a Jeep.

Beka recognized the red Jeep with *KLR* in slanted gold letters across the door. The Jeep belonged to Mr Tavolott, owner of the Kickingbird Lake Resort.

"OK, Jeff!" his aunt hollered back. "You and TJ find the box of food."

"Oh, good," Robbie gushed. "We get to eat before we unpack."

Beka punched his arm. He always forgot rule number six: ghosts don't eat. (They *could*, he liked to remind her, but they didn't *need* to.)

Thatch finished inspecting the boys, then scampered along the curved drive to the Jeep. Beka followed. Listening in on other people's conversations was one nifty advantage to being a ghost – rule number seven.

Aunt Jenny was pretty, Beka thought. Tall (like TJ) but with auburn hair caught up in a clip, leaving curls to tumble down her back. A patch on her shoulder read CANADIAN WILDERNESS TOURS. And she was young. Too young, Beka decided, to be mistaken for the boys' mother.

"No problem," Aunt Jenny was saying through the window of the Jeep.

Mr Tavolott started the engine. "I'll send a crew over to stack firewood in the shed. Nights get nippy this time of year; you'll want to use the fireplace."

Mr Tavolott always fussed over his tenants, making them feel welcome. Beka liked the way he stopped by to greet families who came to stay in the Zuffel house. She often saw his Jeep zipping here and there, making sure the resort was running smoothly.

The Jeep sped away. Aunt Jenny strolled towards the veranda, taking her time, as though she wanted to absorb the warm air and admire the gold and red leaves framing a hazy blue sky.

Or maybe she was avoiding her nephews, Beka wasn't sure.

Inside, the boys had located the food and set the box on the kitchen counter. Meanwhile, they slouched around the table waiting for their aunt.

She arrived, taking stock of the homey kitchen – and the situation. "Is lunch ready?"

TJ gasped. "You want *us* to fix lunch? Mum always makes my lunch at home."

"My mum does, too," Jeff added, looking worried.

Beka groaned.

Robbie acted as if he didn't understand what the fuss was all about.

Aunt Jenny pulled sandwich stuff from the box. "You're not at home now, guys. Out here in the wilderness, it's every cousin for himself."

"The wilderness?" Beka glanced around the remodelled kitchen with its machines for opening cans, washing dishes and heating food in seconds. Things they didn't have fifty years ago. "This is the *wilderness*?"

"Grab the apple juice from the cooler," Aunt

Jenny continued. "And plates and glasses from the cupboards." She paused to peer through the kitchen curtains. "Let's eat outside. It's too nice to stay indoors."

"I checked out the back garden," TJ said. "There's this – this *thing* out among those trees. We can eat there."

"A *thing*?" Aunt Jenny cocked her head at him.

Beka knew instantly what TJ was talking about. The gazebo. She frowned. "Rob, that's *our* gazebo. I don't want to share it with strangers."

"We share the house with strangers," he said. "What's the difference?"

"There's nothing I can do about the house." She moved out of Jeff's way as he pawed through the cupboards. "We've been spoiled, having it all to ourselves for so many years."

Beka watched TJ pack a smaller box with lunch supplies. "But no one's ever invaded our *private* areas – like the gazebo or the attic."

Robbie hustled her and Thatch out of the kitchen door before it closed. "Then don't let these strangers take over. Do something about it."

"Like what?" she asked.

He shrugged. "Use your imagination."

"Come on." TJ raced across the garden, hopping up the gazebo's three steps, and plopping on to the bench. Jeff followed, setting the box of food on the swing that hung in the middle.

"Your *thing*," Aunt Jenny called, "is a gazebo."

"Oh, right." TJ acted as if he'd known it all along.

"Smart guy," Beka mumbled, stepping through the grove of sugarberry trees that hid the gazebo from the house.

"Thatch must have caught a whiff of lunch meat." Robbie tried to keep the dog from sticking his nose into the box. "Try reminding *him* he doesn't need to eat."

"This is great." Aunt Jenny pivoted, taking in the scenery. "While we eat, I'll quiz you on the trees and plants to see if you remember which ones are good for food and medicine, and which to stay away from."

"Aww," Jeff moaned. "We're on our break. Don't give us *another* test."

The agonized look Jeff exchanged with his cousin caught Beka's attention. "Hmmm," she said. "Must have been a fun trip here."

Aunt Jenny placed a fist on each hip. "This is stuff you need to know if you're ever—"

"Lost in the wilderness," TJ finished with mock enthusiasm.

His aunt pretended to pout as she sat stiffly on the swing and opened a bag of wheat bread.

"Tell us about the pond again," Jeff gushed, obviously trying to distract her from launching into another lecture.

"What pond?"

"The one in the magazine article about Kickingbird Lake Resort – the article that gave you the idea to bring us here, and … '*turn my city nephews into outdoor men*,' " he finished, imitating his aunt's voice.

TJ howled, while Aunt Jenny looked miffed.

"Well," she began in a halfhearted manner,

"the article mentioned a certain pond on Mystery Island, known for granting wishes to passers-by."

Pausing, she pulled a schedule from her pocket and studied it. "Over lunch, we're supposed to discuss bird calls, and how you can identify them. Wouldn't you rather hear about *that*?"

"No!" TJ exclaimed.

Jeff's mouth was full, so he shook his head with vigour.

"Ha." Beka nudged Robbie. "They're messing up her schedule."

"Where *is* the pond?" Jeff asked as soon as he swallowed.

Aunt Jenny sipped her apple juice. "No one knows for sure. All who've tried to locate *One Wish Pond*, as it's called, have failed. The irony is, only those who need a wish fulfilled seem to find it."

She waved a hand, as if to end the discussion. "Very mysterious – but I'm sure it's just a local legend."

"I *love* mysteries!" Jeff gestured with both

hands full of food. "When we get to the island, I'm going to find the pond and make a wish."

"No!" Aunt Jenny's abrupt reaction startled Beka, as well as the cousins. "That's not why we're here."

Jeff stopped mid-bite to stare at his aunt.

"I *thought* we were here to have fun," TJ blurted.

If his words hurt Aunt Jenny's feelings, she didn't show it. Instead, she glanced at her watch. "Forget bird calls; let's go on to food. Why do we take peanut butter along when we backpack?"

Beka thought she sounded an awful lot like a school teacher.

"Peanut butter is a quick source of energy," TJ replied in a dull monotone, as if he'd answered the same question a hundred times. "And you can eat it right out of the jar."

"Very good." His aunt looked pleased. "What else do we carry for energy, Jeff?"

He shrugged. "Don't know."

"Trail mix." TJ gave Jeff a smug look. "Nuts, raisins and granola."

"Right." Aunt Jenny passed him a packet of biscuits for dessert. "Jeffrey, you need to pay better attention. If you'd been with me when I led tours into the wilds of the Canadian Yukon, you'd know all these things."

"Don't call me Jeffrey," he said.

Standing, Aunt Jenny took a breath of fresh mountain air, regaining her former enthusiasm. "This will be a *wonderful* weekend, surviving in the great Moosehead wilderness. Just me and my favourite nephews."

"Your *only* nephews," TJ reminded her.

The boys grabbed handfuls of biscuits, then sprinted across the garden to the house.

"Wait!" Aunt Jenny called, but they didn't hear. "Who's supposed to clean up the lunch stuff, and carry everything inside?"

The only ones left to answer were the twins. "You?" Beka offered.

Grumbling under her breath about teamwork and nephews that needed toughening up, Aunt Jenny began throwing things into the box. A half-eaten sandwich fell from TJ's plate.

Falling food was the one thing patient Thatch had been waiting for.

Before Aunt Jenny had time to scoop it up, Thatch made the sandwich disappear faster than anyone could say, "Ghost rule number eight."

Chapter 3
Legends from the Pond

Beka tried to follow Robbie back to the house, but sometimes convincing Thatch to obey was difficult. Especially when food was nearby.

Aunt Jenny knelt to clean up the fallen sandwich. No trace remained, thanks to the ghost dog.

After searching a few moments, she gave up. "Hey, squirrels," she hollered at the near-by branches, "I'd feed you if only you'd ask. Stealing isn't necessary."

Hoisting the box on to one hip, she headed towards the house.

Beka raced Thatch to the cedar deck so

they'd be in position to slip inside when Aunt Jenny opened the door.

Robbie met her in the kitchen. He looked worried.

"What's wrong?"

"You're not going to like it."

"I haven't liked *anything* since our guests arrived."

"The boys picked their bedrooms."

"And one of them chose my old room?" Beka finished for him. "Might be good. My power seems strong in that room. I'll bug him until he flees."

"That's not what happened."

Beka tried to read his mind. Sometimes she could, being his twin, but not today. "What then? One of them picked Thatch's favourite chair?"

"Nope."

Now Beka felt uneasy. "They're sleeping in the gazebo?"

"Sorry, Sis. Try the attic."

"No!" That hadn't crossed Beka's mind. "The attic is *ours*. We've lived there for fifty

21

years. They can't take over my gazebo *and* my attic."

"I know." Robbie tilted his head in sympathy. "I feel the same way. But they've already moved their stuff up there."

"Grrrr," Beka growled. "If they want the attic, they'll have to fight for it." She hugged Thatch for comfort. "And we have a distinct advantage over them. We're ghosts."

The twins hurried upstairs. Afternoon sun slanted across the attic's hardwood floor, making the bedroom area cosy and inviting.

Seeing the cousins throwing their stuff on to the bunk beds and snooping through the dresser and desk made Beka clench her teeth. Why couldn't they choose bedrooms on the lower floors like other Zuffel houseguests?

Jeff and TJ flipped a coin for the top bunk. Jeff won.

"Hey, that's *my* bunk," Beka grumbled. "Mine and Thatch's."

At the sound of his name, Thatch jumped on to the upper bunk.

"No, it's not time for bed," Beka told him,

but let him stay. Might scare Jeff away if the dog accidentally drooled on him when he tried to sleep.

Jeff climbed the ladder and lay down, halfway through Thatch.

Thatch didn't like it. Even *he* knew the bunk belonged to Beka. A low growl vibrated in his throat.

Jeff sprang off the bed, not using the ladder. He hadn't *heard* Thatch growl, but *something* bothered him. "Um," he said, "*you* can have the top bunk, if you like."

"Ha!" Beka laughed. "Thatch spooked him."

TJ yanked jeans from his suitcase. "That's OK. You won the coin toss fair and square."

The cousins unpacked quickly and put their clothes away.

Beka kept blocking their path, making the boys walk "through" her. Normally she hated having someone go through her, but she'd learned it *did* have some effect on the person.

"Are you feeling, um, sudden cold drafts?" Jeff asked.

"Sorta." TJ was intent on shoving his suit-case under the lower bunk.

Jeff shivered. "What do you think it is?"

"It's an old house – *that's* what it is." TJ slammed the last drawer shut. "Now, let's plan our weekend." Unfolding a map, he spread it out on the bed.

"I thought Aunt Jenny had already planned our weekend for us."

"She has, but if we need a break from her 'survival in the wilderness lessons', we can sneak away and go to a film in Juniper." He studied the map. "Look at all the hiking trails. And we can rent bikes or paddleboats."

"I know what *I* want to do." Jeff drew a crumpled paper from his back pocket. "I found this flyer in a kitchen drawer. It tells about One Wish Pond."

"Jeff-rey," TJ said, folding the resort map. "That's just a story somebody made up."

"Don't call me Jeffrey. And it's *not* make-believe." He pointed to one of the stories. "Look at this girl who was dying of some strange disease. She found the pond and wished to be well. And the next time she went to the doctor, he couldn't find anything wrong with her."

TJ was reading over Jeff's shoulder. "It happened way back in 1953. Doctors probably didn't know too much then."

Robbie and Beka exchanged amused glances.

"Then look at this one. A man lost his dog on the island. He wished for the dog to come back. And *while he was making the wish*, his dog came running to him, and they were reunited."

"Coincidence."

"Oh, yeah? Well, it happened a whole *year* after his dog disappeared."

"So the dog survived on the island for a year. Big deal."

Jeff turned the page, searching for another story to convince TJ.

"Guys!" came Aunt Jenny's voice up the stairs. "Time to leave."

"What for?" TJ hollered back, gazing longingly at the list of activities he'd rather be doing.

"A ranger talk. At the amphitheatre."

TJ collapsed on the floor. "Give us a break. We're on holiday."

Jeff stuffed the flyer about One Wish Pond back into his pocket. "Doesn't Aunt Jenny remind you of Mr Mendez?"

"Ha," TJ laughed. "The teacher who never stopped teaching?"

"Yeah, you'd say 'good morning,' and he'd teach you about weather balloons."

"Or tell you where the phrase *good morning* came from."

"Boys! Get down here, or we'll be late."

The cousins trudged downstairs, the twins and Thatch on their heels.

"Do we *have* to go?" Jeff asked.

"Yes," Aunt Jenny said, lacing her hiking boots.

"How can you make us listen to a boring lecture when we're off from school?" TJ added.

"You won't be bored," she said, hustling them out of the door. "Trust me."

"*Trust me* is what you said when you took

the wrong exit on the way to Juniper." TJ grinned to soften his comment.

The boys jumped off the veranda and leaned against their aunt's car.

She waved a map at them. "The amphitheatre isn't far; we're walking."

Jeff groaned for the umpteenth time since he arrived. "She's gonna kill us," he mumbled, shuffling along the drive.

"What a couple of babies," Beka said, heading back to the veranda.

"Hey, Sis, you're coming with us, aren't you?"

"You mean you're going to the amphitheatre, too?" Beka glanced at the group heading down Deer Creek Road. "Why?"

"Why not?" Robbie held Thatch's collar to keep the dog from bounding away. "See? Even Thatch wants to go."

"But I've *borrowed* a whole stack of books from the library." She loved to "check out" books from the library in Juniper, although no one there suspected they had a ghost patron.

"Please, Raz?" Robbie said, using the

nickname formed from their shared initials.

Beka could never say *no* to her brother when he used that tone of voice. "OK, I'll go," she said with a sigh. "Maybe it'll give me time to make up as many scary reasons as it takes to get these cousins out of my attic."

Chapter 4
Chasing a Ghost Dog

The group hurried up Aspen Lane towards Moosehead National Park.

Aunt Jenny placed a hand on each nephew's head and tried to straighten their hair – pointless on such a windy afternoon. "When you're out in the wilderness," she began, "what do you do the minute – no, the *second* – you realize you're lost?"

"Dial 911," TJ said without hesitation.

"Huh?" Beka glanced at her brother. "What does *that* mean?"

Robbie shrugged.

"There aren't any phones in the wilderness, dear."

"Then you stop at the first McDonald's you come to and ask directions," Jeff offered.

"OK, wise guys." Aunt Jenny looked disappointed. "Don't come crying to me if you forget what to do."

"If we can find *you*, then we're not lost," TJ told her.

"Good point," Jeff added.

"Will you *please* be serious?"

TJ picked up a rock and heaved it up the road.

Thatch took off like a firecracker, but couldn't find the rock when it landed in a pile of others just like it.

"When you first realize you're lost," TJ said, "you find a big tree and sit underneath it."

"Then what?" Aunt Jenny asked.

"Stay there until you're found."

"Why?"

"Because if you keep walking, you might wander in the wrong direction and make it harder for anyone to find you."

"Very good. You *do* listen to your ol' aunt sometimes."

Arriving at the tollbooth under the arch, Aunt Jenny waved a pass to show the rangers they were guests of the resort.

North of Alpine Lodge was the amphitheatre, with its indoor/outdoor stages. Today's event was inside. The group joined the flow of tourists who were quickly filling the seats that formed a half-circle in front of the stage.

TJ wanted to sit in the back row. Jeff wanted to sit in the front. They compromised and picked a row in the middle.

The seats around the group were full. The only way the twins could join them was to "share" a seat with someone else.

"Let's not," Beka said, dropping to her knees at one side of the stage, and clicking her tongue at Thatch to sit next to her.

Robbie hesitated. "We can't listen to their conversations from here."

"I don't like sharing the same space with people. It gives me the heebie-jeebies."

Lights clicked off, washing the theatre in darkness. Robbie gave up his argument and joined Beka on the edge of the stage.

Classical music began to play; then Ranger Parella's voice boomed from somewhere in the dark, welcoming all guests of Kickingbird Lake Resort to her afternoon lecture.

A machine began to whir, throwing light on to a giant screen as it descended, covering the back wall of the stage.

"Wow," Beka whispered. "Modern magic."

Pictures flashed on to the screen while the ranger narrated. Scenes of Moosehead National Park awakening in the spring with blooming flowers amid melting snow and trickling streams. Baby bears, fawns and raccoons tumbled and chased across the screen, making laughter echo from the audience.

The scene changed to summer. Hikers explored trails, pitched tents and cooked over open fires. Sailing-boats glistened on Kickingbird Lake; swimmers waved from the shore. Tourists shopped at the outdoor Moosehead Mall, and splashed in the pool.

Autumn lit the screen on fire. Hillsides changed from green to glittery gold and russet red. Campers poked marshmallows on to willow sticks and roasted them over campfires.

Beka blinked as colour gave way to the whiteness of winter. Skiers *schussed* down slopes of the Walrus Mountain ski run. Kids were tobogganing in the foothills. Winter rabbits, as white as the drifts, loped through fresh powder, leaving their unique footprints.

The audience *oohed* and *ahhed* in all the right places.

The scene changed to Mr Tavolott, sitting in a comfortable chair by the huge rock fireplace in Alpine Lodge, sipping hot chocolate and snacking on popcorn.

As he began to tell listeners the history of Moosehead and the resort, the scraggly shadow of a dog bounded back and forth across the screen.

Sniggers skittered through the audience.

Ranger Parella jumped from her spot at the microphone to chase away the intruder. Halfway across the stage, she stopped abruptly, whirling in a circle. "What the—?" the twins heard her whisper.

Beka was enjoying the show so much, it took a minute for the truth to wriggle into her consciousness.

The ranger was chasing a dog who simply wasn't there.

The ranger was chasing a ghost dog.

Chapter 5
Nature Salad

Popcorn!

The camera had zoomed close to the bowl from which Mr Tavolott was snacking. White puffs of popcorn filled the screen, larger than life, tempting one and all.

Especially a ghost dog who dearly loved popcorn. Thatch used to chase kernels when Beka tossed them across a room. And he loved to crunch each salty bite.

Now the shadow-dog was on his hind legs, begging for a treat as he blocked the image of Mr Tavolott, who continued his story unaware of the fact that he was being upstaged.

Beka wondered why Thatch's shadow could

be seen at all. She pushed aside the confusion in her mind. Racing across the stage, she ducked low so *her* image wouldn't block the moving pictures as well.

"Look!" Robbie shouted from the sidelines.

Beka gaped at the screen. Her shadow was *not* there. Only Thatch's.

Grabbing the dog's collar, she yanked him away.

The audience watched in stunned silence as the dog was pulled off stage. By someone who was there, yet wasn't.

Loud discussions erupted over what they'd just observed.

Robbie wrapped his arms around Thatch to hold him back. "I don't get it," he whispered. "Rules of the world stay the same. Yet ghost rules slip and slide and don't stay put."

Beka knew what he was trying to say. "You mean – why could everyone see Thatch's shadow, and not mine?"

He nodded.

The only answer she could offer was that sometimes Thatch could do things they couldn't. (See ghost rule number four.)

Ranger Parella calmed the audience by pretending nothing odd had just happened. She simply hurried on with her lecture.

As the lights brightened a notch, the ranger stepped to a podium and launched into a story about a girl who became lost in the wilderness, but didn't go hungry because she knew how to make a nature salad.

Each ingredient flashed on to the screen for easy identification as the ranger listed them: dandelion greens, chicory, milkweed shoots, sweet clover and pepper grass, along with a few sand plums on the side.

"To go with it," Ranger Parella said, "add a glass of water from any stream. Oak leaves will purify the water so you won't get sick, and charcoal from your fire will sweeten and freshen the taste."

"Nifty," Robbie exclaimed.

Beka thought it strange to graze among the plants in the wild like an animal. Yet, she guessed she'd do it if she were hungry enough.

When the show ended, the twins waited by

an exit gate for the cousins and Aunt Jenny –
who was bubbling over with excitement at
all the great survival tips Ranger Parella had
shared.

"Can we go home now?" Jeff asked, clicking
on a torch to beam the way. "And get some
real food to snack on?"

Beka took hold of a handful of dry grass
alongside the road. She concentrated until
the grass moved in her hand, meaning that
now she had control over it. As she yanked it
out by the roots, the blades became invisible.

Catching up with Jeff, she sprinkled it on to
his shoulder. "Snack on this," she teased. As
the grass left her hand, it sparked a muted
yellow, becoming visible as it rained down on
Jeff's jacket.

"Hey!" He stopped in the middle of the
road to brush the grass away. Then he aimed
his torch towards the overhanging branches to
see where the grass had fallen from.

"You're bad," Robbie told his sister, following close to the group to take advantage of the
torch.

"I'm just getting warmed up," Beka said. "Remember where Jeff is sleeping tonight? In *my* bunk. Mine and Thatch's. And TJ is sleeping in *yours*."

"You sound like the littlest bear in *Goldilocks*," Robbie laughed, sing-songing, " 'Somebody's been sleeping in my bed.' "

"Well, I don't like it." Beka felt miffed. "If Aunt Jenny is worried about her dear nephew surviving in the great outdoors, just wait until she learns he can't even survive one night in the Zuffel attic."

Chapter 6
It Was Done
in the Attic…

"Let's play a game before we go to bed."
Jeff was speaking to TJ, yet his gaze
travelled the attic, across the high rafters to the
shadowed stairwell and into every dark corner.

"He doesn't seem eager to turn out the
lights tonight," Robbie said.

"Heh, heh, heh," Beka added.

The floor lamp next to the dresser offered
the only light, creating a warm, glowing circle
in the middle of the room, but leaving the rest
of the area shadowed in darkness.

"My mum wouldn't let me bring any video
games," TJ answered. "Even after she found
out the house had a TV. She said this was my
holiday from civilization."

"That's OK; I brought Cluedo." Jeff scrambled off the bed and dug through a duffel bag he hadn't unpacked yet.

"Cluedo?" Beka repeated. "I don't suppose people play Monopoly any more."

Kneeling on the braided rug, Jeff opened the game and set it up. "I want to be Colonel Mustard."

"You were Colonel Mustard last time. *I* get him this time."

"It was my idea to play. You can be … Miss Scarlet." Jeff tee-heed the way someone named "Miss Scarlet" might.

TJ ignored him, picking up a purple piece. "I'd rather be Professor Plum." He tossed the mustard-coloured piece to his cousin.

"Can *we* play, too?" Robbie joined the boys on the floor, making room for Thatch. "Lie down," he commanded.

Thatch, whose curiosity about the game grew by the second, whined, but obeyed his master, lying just out of paw-reach from the board.

Jeff dealt cards while TJ scattered the "weapons".

Beka read the rules in the overturned lid of the box. "This sounds like fun," she said. "*I'll* be Miss Scarlet, and Rob, you can be Reverend Green."

"Who does Thatch get to be?"

"Knowing Thatch, he won't be a person at all. He'll be one of the weapons – ha!"

The game began. Beka soon became bored since she couldn't take a turn. Standing, she circled the group around the edge of the braided rug.

"When we were at the amphitheatre," Jeff began, "where do you think the dog-shadow came from?"

"Don't know. Don't care." TJ concentrated on the game.

"The dog-shadow is right here," Beka whispered. "Why don't you ask him?"

"It was done in the kitchen," TJ said. "By Mrs Peacock. With the candlestick."

Jeff flipped the candlestick card on to the table.

"Rats," TJ mumbled.

Beka continued her circle. "It was done in

the attic," she whispered into Jeff's ear. "By the twins. With a ghost dog."

Robbie laughed. "You really hate these guys being here, don't you?"

"Doesn't it bother you?"

"I think it's rather entertaining." Robbie sprawled on the floor, using Thatch's rump for a pillow.

"I want them gone," Beka grumbled.

"Then give it your best shot."

"I'm *trying*." She continued to circle, chanting "It was done in the attic, it was done in the attic," in Jeff's ear.

"It's your turn." TJ snapped his fingers in front of Jeff's face. "Come on; pay attention. You keep day-dreaming."

"Did you just hear something?"

"Like what?"

"Like someone talking. Only real quiet so you can barely hear them?"

TJ listened for a moment. "Maybe Aunt Jenny is talking on the phone downstairs."

"There isn't a phone downstairs. This is a holiday home."

"Oh. Then it's the wind. Blowing around this creaky old house." TJ acted exasperated. "Take your turn, cuz."

Jeff tossed the die and moved his piece into the library. He cleared his throat. "It was done in the attic. By—"

"Hold it. There *is* no attic in this game. Your piece is in the library."

"Did I say attic?"

"Yup."

"Sorry. It was done in the ... the library. By the twins."

"What? Who are the twins?"

"I don't know."

TJ slammed his cards on to the board. "That's it. I quit. You're being weird." He stood, kicked off his shoes, and climbed into the lower bunk, clothes and all. "Turn out the light when you're finished."

Jeff remained on the floor. "You're not going to *sleep* now, are you?"

"It's almost midnight."

Jeff didn't answer.

"Ah, I get it." TJ rolled on to his side.

"You're afraid of the dark. Is that it? You want to leave a night-light on?"

Jeff cringed as his cousin laughed.

"No. I'm not afraid of the dark. It's just … it's this attic. There's something strange about it. Don't you think?"

"I think there's something strange about *you*." He yawned. "Leave the lamp on all night, if it makes you feel better." With that, TJ pulled the covers over his head and said no more.

Jeff put the game away. Slowly. Then he climbed to the upper bunk and lay down on top of the quilt.

"Guess we can call it a night," Robbie said. "I'm going downstairs to my old bedroom. Why don't you do the same?"

"And miss all the fun?" Beka hurried to the window seat where she kept her library books. She returned, flashing a cover in Robbie's direction.

"*Tales to Keep You Awake All Night*," he read.

"I'm going to read Jeff some bedtime

stories." Beka flipped through the pages. "Looks like it will take most of the night to read the whole book out loud to him."

Robbie said good night and headed downstairs.

Beka and Thatch climbed to the top bunk. She sat at the end of the bed, while Thatch stretched out alongside Jeff.

Jeff's eyes remained open, and the lamp stayed on.

Beka began: "Once, there was a boy who lost his way in the woods. As he wandered, searching for ... One Wish Pond, strange noises scared him. His name was ... Jeff." Beka smiled at her own cleverness. "Jeff is the name of *every* character in all of tonight's spooky stories."

Chapter 7
A Change of Plans

"Finish your breakfast so we can pack for today's big adventure." Aunt Jenny's enthusiasm overflowed like the water in both canteens she was filling at the kitchen sink.

TJ shovelled down his cereal, but Jeff's eyes remained closed. A spoon rested in mid-air, half-way to his mouth.

"Jeff had all the adventures he could handle last night," Beka said, smirking.

Aunt Jenny nudged his shoulder. "What's wrong, Jeffrey?"

"Huh?" He flinched, looking startled, then relieved when he saw where he was. "Oh, I didn't get much sleep last night."

"Why not? Aren't the bunks comfortable?"

"Yeah. I just — well, I kept having night-mares."

"Like what?" TJ scoffed. "Getting done in by Miss Scarlet?"

"Like, terrible things kept happening to me in every dream. And all these horrible creatures knew my name."

"Oh, poor dear." Aunt Jenny gave him an awkward kiss on top of his head. "You should have come downstairs. I would have put you to bed in another room, and stayed until you fell asleep."

"That's what Mum would have done, too," Jeff mumbled.

"Is the *poor dear* homesick?" TJ whispered. Aunt Jenny heard, and motioned for him not to tease.

"Well, forget last night," she said, sounding as bright as the sun peeking through the kitchen curtains. "Today's going to be one of the best days of your lives." She lifted a back-pack to estimate its weight. "Today you'll put to use all the survival skills I've taught you."

"Camping on Mystery Island is *not* the same as trekking through the Canadian Yukon," TJ reminded her.

"I know." Aunt Jenny gazed at the ceiling, a dreamy look softening her face. "Did I ever tell you about the weekend we packed as far north as Old Crow on the Porcupine River?"

"A million times," TJ moaned. "The temperature never rose above zero, your water supply froze, and you survived for three days on nothing but peanut butter and raisins."

"Oh." She acted disappointed, not getting to tell the story herself. "Well, guys, you gotta be tough. Can't be stopped by a little cold, or hunger, or—"

"Nightmares," TJ threw in.

"True," Aunt Jenny agreed.

Jeff dipped his head and finished his soggy cereal.

Suddenly Robbie and Thatch dashed into the kitchen from the butler's pantry.

"Good morning," Beka said.

"Sorry we're late for breakfast," Robbie teased. "Thatch and I were playing chase upstairs on the landing." He glanced at her. "Well, it's nice to see you in such a good mood. Your all-night haunting session must have worked."

"It not only worked, but the cousins are off on a camping trip today, which means we have the attic all to ourselves."

At the word "camping", Thatch began to dance around the kitchen in anticipation. His toenails clicked so loudly on the tiles, Beka was surprised no one but them could hear.

"I forgot," she said. "*Camping* is a word he knows." Beka remembered all the times they'd camped when Thatch was a puppy, and how much fun he'd had chasing about in the woods, protecting them from every shadow.

"Camping," Robbie mumbled. "Sounds nifty. We haven't camped in years." He joined Thatch's dance, twirling him around by his front paws. "We can't stay here while everyone else goes off to have fun, Sis. Let's go with them."

Beka wrinkled her nose. So much for a long peaceful evening in a quiet house.

"Try this." Aunt Jenny held the backpack while TJ strapped it on.

"Is it too heavy?"

"Nope."

Beka figured he'd say *no* whether it was true or not – to avoid another lecture from his aunt on being tough.

"I've only packed the essentials," she told him. "You're the tallest, so you can carry more."

"But Jeff *weighs* more."

Aunt Jenny wisely chose not to answer his comment. Jeff's nasty look was answer enough. Picking up a quickly scribbled list, she studied it for a moment.

Beka peeked over her shoulder to read it:

1. Breakfast
2. Get packs ready
3. Showers
4. Call for ride to marina

"Time for showers," she said. "Dress warmly. I've packed extra clothes, but it's chilly this morning and will be cold tonight. Don't forget to brush your teeth." She stopped to laugh. "Oh, no, I sound like your mothers."

"You can say that again," the boys chimed.

"Hut, hut." She clapped her hands. "Let's go, guys. It takes time to get to the island, find a good spot and set up camp."

Jeff headed for the door.

TJ's eyes stayed on his aunt. "Wait."

Jeff obeyed.

"Where's *your* pack, Aunt Jenny?"

"My pack?" A guilty expression reddened her face. "I don't need a pack. I'm not going."

"What?" Jeff's voice squeaked up an octave.

"I knew it." TJ scowled.

"You're not camping with us?" Jeff stammered. "But you *brought* us here to teach us how to survive under any circumstances."

"And this is one of those circumstances." Aunt Jenny calmly carried dishes to the sink. "If I go, I'll end up doing everything for you. Look at this." She held up Jeff's cereal bowl to make her point. "I'm doing it right now.

You've been quick learners when we've *talked* about the wilderness. But the only way you'll really learn is by *doing* it. By yourselves. Without your aunt there to do it for you."

The boys didn't look convinced, so she continued. "You have everything you need right here." She tapped a backpack. "And here." She added a tap to the side of TJ's head. "And you'll have lots more fun without me tagging along."

"Y-you're really sending us to M-Mystery Island alone?" Jeff made it sound as foreboding as if she were sending them off to Mars.

"Yup."

Beka knew Robbie was grinning at her but she ignored him. Mystery Island was *not* the safest place to send two bumbling cousins on their own.

The CAMP AT YOUR OWN RISK signs popped into her mind, warning campers of steep drop-offs, dense forests, paths leading nowhere and a good share of wild animals.

Then there was the other danger. Beka tried

not to think about it – the uneven coastline causing tides to shift unexpectedly, or the fact that the unpredictable waters off Mystery Island were the scene of the "mishap" suffered by the ghost twins of Kickingbird Lake some fifty years ago.

She'd never gone back. And did she really want to go back now? With two city boys who didn't know what they were doing?

Robbie's anxious grin and Thatch's eager whining overruled her inner turmoil.

Chapter 8
And Then
They Were Off…

"The van is here!" Aunt Jenny yelled from the hall.

The boys trudged down the stairway as if they were off to their doom instead of a fun camping trip.

"Hut, hut," their aunt called.

Meanwhile, the twins and Thatch had already climbed into the open side of the shuttle van and taken seats in the back.

Beka recognized the driver. Eric the lifeguard. Now he was Eric the shuttle driver. The teenage junior rangers who worked for Mr Tavolott filled in anywhere they were needed.

And, if she remembered correctly, this was

the weekend the pool closed for the season. Yesterday's dip in temperature had remained, sending everyone out today in jackets and sweaters.

Aunt Jenny hugged her nephews goodbye as they climbed into the shuttle. The boys didn't have much to say.

She did: "Pick a campsite sheltered by trees in case it's windy. Build a fire as soon as you get there and keep it going. Gather twice as much wood as you think you're going to need, and—"

"We know, we know." TJ's look curtailed her list of instructions.

"I can't tell if he's angry at her for not going with them," Beka said, "or eager to get away from her."

"A little of both?" Robbie answered.

"I think Aunt Jenny is making a big mistake. If she'd read up on the history of Mystery Island, she'd never let the boys go over there alone." That gave Beka an idea. "Hey, maybe we should scatter the flyers around the house where she'll see them."

"Too late," Robbie said as Eric slammed the door and climbed into the driver's seat.

The shuttle jerked, crunching on gravel in the drive.

"Wave goodbye to Aunt Jenny," Beka said, holding Thatch up to the back window and shaking his paw.

"Woof," Thatch said.

Aunt Jenny was waving and yelling last-minute tips, but the boys obviously weren't ready to forgive her yet.

Morning frost tipped tree branches along the way to the lake. Kickingbird was a year-round resort, so autumn weather didn't mean that fewer tourists crowded the roads.

Instead, Eric had to drive slow because of bus-loads of people coming to watch the turning of the leaves.

Or to take walking tours along the lake while rangers gave talks on how animals adapt to the change in seasons.

Or to sip hot spiced cider by the giant fire-place in Alpine Lodge.

As the shuttle passed under the entry arch, traffic thinned out. Winding its way around the lake, the van came to a stop at the marina, and the group tumbled out.

Eric opened the back to unload the boys' packs. "I'm supposed to get you fixed up with a canoe and see you off," he explained.

Beka's feelings of dread began the moment she stepped on to the marina. Why? Was it memories of that long-ago day she climbed into a canoe off this same marina, yet never returned?

Or an omen that the cousins had no business being out on the lake – or on Mystery Island – alone?

After a crash course in canoeing from Eric – with the promise of "anyone can do it" – the cousins stepped gingerly into a canoe, secured to the dock by a hefty rope.

Eric placed one pack in each end of the boat for balance, then handed out paddles, showing the boys how to row. (Or *pull, lift, push, lower,* as he called it.)

"Do we take our own canoe, or go with

them?" Beka asked.

"I was wondering the same thing."

"If we go with them, we'll be right there in case … you know … in case something happens."

"Right." Robbie hustled Thatch on to the dock. "Think fast," he said, hopping into the boys' canoe with the dog.

Beka followed, amazed that their movements did not rock the boat in the slightest. "Should I sit in front?" she asked. "For balance?"

"We're weightless," Robbie reminded her. "Doesn't matter."

When Beka settled into the canoe next to Jeff, he stiffened. Was he sensitive to her presence since she'd bothered him all night in the attic?

Then they were off, shooting across Kickingbird Lake like old times.

Beka gazed towards Mystery Island, looming in the distance like a forgotten enemy. Squinting, she spotted the old pier, tumbling down now from lack of upkeep.

Thatch barked excitedly as they drew near land.

Robbie relaxed against TJ's pack. "Letting someone else do all the rowing is nice."

The canoe came to rest at a new dock. TJ hopped out and threw a loop of rope around a wood post to secure the canoe, as Eric had instructed him.

Jeff handed over the packs then climbed to shore.

Thatch scrambled on to land, instantly dashing off into the heavily wooded forest.

"Thatch!" Panic touched Beka's throat. "I should have held on to his collar."

"He'll be all right," Robbie said, helping her out of the canoe. "This is his old stomping ground, remember?"

Beka trudged on to the rocky shore, eyes and ears alert to danger.

What was making the hair on the back of her neck rise? All those spooky legends that refused to die? Like the ones about One Wish Pond?

Or was it the idea of spending an entire

night on Mystery Island?

They'd always camped on the mainland, not here. Their favourite spot was Zuffel Rock on the north shore. (Robbie had named the rock formation after himself.)

But there was something eerie about the island. Every time they'd picnicked or hiked here, Beka had found herself glancing over one shoulder.

"Thatch," she whispered, needing her dog for comfort and protection. "Please, please come back."

Chapter 9
Wishes and Mosquitoes

The cousins struggled into their oversized backpacks.

TJ made sure the canoe was secured to the post, then the boys stood quietly on the rocky shore, facing the dense forest, teeming with life and unfamiliar noises.

Beka remembered how awestruck she'd been the first time she'd visited the island.

TJ shifted his pack and took one bold step forward. "Mystery Island," he exclaimed, swiping at a mosquito, "here we come."

"All by ourselves," Jeff added. "Thanks to Aunt Jenny."

"Aww, we don't need her. Besides, we've got

the next best thing." Reaching into his jacket, TJ pulled out a checklist. "We've got Aunt Jenny's answers without having to listen to her questions."

"I don't care what's on Aunt Jenny's check-list," Jeff snapped. "The first thing *I'm* going to do is find the pond, then—"

"Pond? *What* pond?"

Jeff looked at his cousin as if he'd asked which sun was shining. "One Wish Pond. You know, the one that grants you anything you want."

Now it was TJ's turn to look at Jeff as though he were crazy. "You've got to be kidding. You believe in that fairy tale?"

"It's *not* a fairy tale." Jeff wiggled about, acting uncomfortable with the backpack and his cousin's accusation. "Just ask the girl who was chased by some ... some *monster* in the dark. She got to the pool, and wished for safety, then—"

"Then what?"

"Lightning struck. Out of nowhere. It fizzled something right behind her. When she looked, all she saw was this burned-out tree in the shape of a horrible monster – with limbs like this." Jeff demonstrated by spreading his arms and fingers, trying to look like a horrible tree monster.

TJ howled.

"What's so funny?"

"She was chased by a *tree*?"

"No, no, no." Jeff sighed. "Forget the story." Miffed, he hiked towards the beginnings of an overgrown path that disappeared around a rocky bend. "You'll thank me later when we find the pond, and all our wishes come true."

TJ caught up with him. "Yeah? I thought your magic pond granted *one* wish, not *all* your wishes."

"True. But my one wish will be for all the other wishes I want." Jeff gave TJ a smug look. "Brilliant, huh?"

His cousin was quiet, pondering the idea, while smacking a few mosquitoes.

"*Brilliant* is not the right word," Beka groaned. One Wish Pond was not news to her. She'd heard the legends many times. Yet Jeff was forgetting his aunt's words. *Only those who seemed to need the pond found it.* Jeff's "need" was more like "greed".

"Hey," Robbie said, trailing behind the others. "I think I remember the story Jeff was trying to tell. Only that's not exactly how it happened."

"Yeah." Beka stepped around a washed-out area of the path. "The girl wasn't chased by a monster. It was a bobcat, right?"

"Right. The island had got overrun with bobcats in those days, and the forest service had to move most of them to the high country."

"And lightning *did* strike the tree behind the girl," Beka added. "But what the legend fails to mention is that *thunder* is what scared the cat away."

Robbie caught up with her and the boys. "The *true* version of the story isn't nearly as interesting as Jeff's telling."

Beka agreed. Funny how events turned into stories, then legends, with the lines blurred between fact and fiction. She often wondered how different the *true* story of her and Robbie and Thatch had become after many retellings by different people over the years. (That is, if people talked about them at all…)

The cousins hiked in silence. Soon, the trail took a sharp curve uphill. In minutes, they were panting for breath.

For the twins, the climb was easy. Ghosts could hike all day and night and never grow tired, or need to sleep. (Another ghost rule, Beka thought, although she'd forgotten what number she was on. Was it nine?)

At the top of the next rise, Robbie stopped. "You're worried about Thatch, aren't you?"

"You can tell?" Beka had been peering behind every rock and tree they'd passed. "Yeah, I'm worried. Thatch usually tags along with us."

"I'm worried, too," Robbie said. "Why don't you stay with the guys, and I'll go look for him? He took off in the opposite direction."

Beka wasn't thrilled about Robbie deserting her. "You're going to leave me alone with the bickering cousins?"

He patted her on the shoulder. "If they get into trouble and you need help, just holler, and I'll come running."

"But how will you find us?"

"Listen."

Beka listened. The boys were making enough noise to be heard by the fish in Kickingbird Lake.

"Good point," she said.

Robbie disappeared down the trail. Watching him leave gave Beka an odd sensation. She and Robbie – and Thatch – were together constantly. She rarely found herself alone.

Alone.

Here on Mystery Island.

With two annoying cousins who were now arguing over whether to stop and set up camp, or keep looking for a wishing pond – which Beka felt sure didn't exist.

Chapter 10
Lions and Tigers and Bears, Oh My!

"**W**e're not following Aunt Jenny's checklist," TJ grumbled. "And you know she's going to quiz us on it all the way home. If we don't give the right answers, we're in for twenty more lectures. Plus she'll tell our parents we didn't cooperate."

He yanked on Jeff's shoulder strap. "Remember our mums' warning? We'd get into big trouble if we didn't cooperate with Aunt Jenny?"

Jeff nodded. "Let's stop for lunch." He put on the brakes so abruptly, TJ smashed into him, and Beka smashed into TJ. Or rather, smashed *through* him.

Jeff slipped off his pack and headed for a flat, sunny rock before his cousin could answer.

"Hey, we're supposed to set up camp *first* — before we do anything else." TJ waited, as if his words would convince Jeff to give up on eating and return to the path. "The weather might change," he added, "and we need time to gather firewood for the night."

"But I'm hungry *now*." Jeff settled on to the rock and unzipped his pack. "And tired, too. I didn't get much sleep last night, remember?"

TJ looked annoyed. "You're *always* hungry." Giving in, he shrugged off his pack and sat next to his cousin.

Beka climbed a nearby chestnut tree, just for something to do. Or was it to see if she could spot Robbie and Thatch over the tree-tops?

"Read me Aunt Jenny's checklist while I eat," Jeff said between bites.

TJ pulled the paper from his pocket and unfolded it. " 'Number one,' " he read. " 'Make sure canoe is secured well in case a storm tugs at the line.' " He glanced up. "Did that. 'Next, hike well into the area to get a taste of your surroundings.' "

He shot a sarcastic look at his cousin. "You're the one getting a taste of our surroundings."

Jeff ripped open a carton of juice as his answer.

" 'Next,' " TJ continued, " 'keep an eye out for the best place to set up camp – flat, free of rocks and tree stumps, near a source of water.' "

He paused, reading ahead. " 'Don't camp *too* near water because the air is colder, there are more insects, and you might be in the pathway of animals coming to drink at night.' "

"Animals?" Jeff stopped chewing and glanced about.

"You're such a city boy," TJ teased. "Didn't you think there'd be animals around our camp?"

"Well, yeah, squirrels and rabbits and birds. But Aunt Jenny wouldn't warn us about *those* kinds of animals. She must be warning us about *bigger* animals."

TJ pretended to be scared. "Lions and tigers and bears, oh my!"

"Y-you don't think there are any of ... of *those* around, do you?"

"Why don't you ask your magic pond?"

Beka balanced on a branch above them, blocking out their arguments while she studied the nifty way mosquitoes flew through her arm without landing – or biting.

Jeff consoled himself with more food.

TJ buried his head in the checklist. " 'Next step: sweep the chosen campsite clean with a broom made of evergreen boughs. Unroll sleeping mats and inflate them.' "

"Shouldn't we set up the tent first?"

TJ gave him a dull look. "There *is* no tent."

"What? I thought I was carrying the food so you could carry the tent."

"Don't you *ever* listen to Aunt Jenny? We're sleeping under the stars tonight because she thinks it will make us *tougher*."

"I don't want to be tough. I want to be warm and dry and safe. What if it rains? Or what if we need protection from ... from something?"

"From a burned-out tree monster? Ha!"

Jeff mumbled a sarcastic response Beka didn't catch.

TJ finished laughing at his own cleverness. "Remember the Saturday we spent building that shelter out of twigs and branches and a tarpaulin in Grandpa's backyard? The shelter Aunt Jenny called a *wickiup?*"

"A wickiup?" Beka repeated.

Jeff nodded.

"Why do you think Aunt Jenny taught us that? In case we ran into danger in Grandpa's backyard?"

"Very funny."

"Listen to this: 'If the smell of rain or snow is in the air, or if any night animals are around, build a wickiup the way I taught you,'" TJ read. "*That's* what we're supposed to do if we want to keep warm and dry and safe."

"*Night* animals? You're kidding." Jeff looked stunned, as if he'd planned on taking a taxi to the nearest motel if the weather turned, or a bear showed up. He stopped eating for a minute to sniff the air. "What does rain or snow smell like?"

"Guess we'll find out if it happens." TJ chuckled at the forlorn look on his cousin's face. "You don't think Aunt Jenny sent us over to enjoy ourselves, do you? She sent us over here to get tough and learn how to survive."

Jeff pulled his fourth chocolate bar from the pack and peeled off the paper, pondering TJ's words.

"Toss me one of those," TJ said. "I'm getting hungry now."

"Um, this is the last one."

"You ate *all* the chocolate?"

"Sorry." Jeff turned his eyes away. "Do you want the rest of mine?"

"Naw." TJ thrust the checklist into his pocket without folding it. "Hand me the trail mix."

Jeff pulled out an empty bag.

"You ate that, too? You ate *all* of our food?"

"No. Just a few things. I was really hungry."

"Jeff-rey! That food was supposed to last all

weekend." Grabbing Jeff's pack, he sorted what was left. "You ate both our lunches and half of tonight's dinner."

Jeff crumpled the bag into a ball, hiding the evidence. "We can always make a nature salad," he offered. "Like Ranger Parella said."

"*You* can eat plants. *I'm* not." TJ snatched the remaining food, and shoved it into his own pack. "Thanks a lot, cuz. You've eaten our food, got us lost, and thrown us way off schedule."

"We're not lost," Jeff mumbled.

TJ uncapped a small jar of peanut butter and scooped some on to his finger to eat. Putting it away, he scrambled to his feet. "Time to stop looking for that stupid pond and start looking for a good campsite."

"But—"

"I don't care about your magic pond. I don't want to be wandering around after dark with no camp, no fire and no food."

"Just let me look in *one* more place," Jeff begged, as if trying to regain his cousin's approval. "See those birds?" He pointed over the treetops to a tall pine. A half–dozen birds perched in the branches or fluttered about.

"Yeah. So what?"

"Follow me there. I know we have to leave the trail, but I'll keep the tree in sight; I promise."

TJ scrunched his face. "Why should we hike over there?"

"When the birds hang around a tree, it's a sign water is nearby."

"How do you know?"

Jeff gave TJ a mock disgusted look. "Don't you *ever* listen to Aunt Jenny?"

Beka waited before shimmying down the chestnut to follow the boys off the path into the rocky undergrowth. This was *not* a good idea. They'd already hiked deep into the forest. With the sameness of scenery, getting lost was easy.

Too easy.

Besides, they hadn't been using the compasses dangling from the zips on their packs. They had no idea in which direction they were hiking – or which direction would lead them back to the canoe.

"Hey!" Beka yelled. "Don't *either* of you listen to Aunt Jenny?" She knew they couldn't hear, but she felt like shouting with frustration at the poor choices they were making. "Didn't your aunt warn you never to leave the path?"

Pushing off from the branch, she dropped twenty feet to the ground, landing smoothly on both feet. "Ha!" she crowed. "Bet you guys can't do *that*."

Chapter 11
Home Sweet Home

The going was rough. Vines and weeds tangled about the boys' legs.

The side of the hill was strewn with hidden rocks. Fat shrubs, sharp cactuses and prickly grasses sent the group on a zigzag trail.

Finally, they broke through the undergrowth. "Way to go," TJ panted. He balanced on a rock overlooking a fast-moving stream. The pine with the fluttering birds grew on the opposite bank.

"I *told* you we'd find water here," Jeff said, acting smug.

"This is a stream – not a pond. Don't you know the difference? Next you'll tell me this is a *magic* stream."

TJ yanked his jacket sleeve back to peer at his watch. "Look how much time we've wasted. And now the sky is cloudy, which means darkness will come sooner. We should be relaxing by a fire right now, planning what to eat for dinner – or what's *left* of our dinner."

"OK, I give up." Jeff tossed a twig into the stream and watched it swirl away. "Let's go back to the path and see where it leads. Or," he added, brightening, "we can go back to the shore and camp by the canoe – away from, um, away from *things*."

"Things? You mean animals? Aunt Jenny said they go to water at night. Why would the shore of a lake be safer than the bank of a stream?"

"Oh, right." Jeff headed up the hill they'd just stumbled down. He flailed his arms to ward off branches and flying insects as he struggled over nature's obstacles.

With a heavy sigh, TJ followed.

Beka imitated his sigh. "I feel like I'm travelling with Laurel and Hardy," she grumbled.

Thirty minutes passed, with no sign of the path.

Beka had sensed early on that they were heading in the wrong direction. She should've distracted the cousins, then herded them the right way.

Unfortunately, she didn't know the right way. She hadn't paid any more attention when the boys left the path than they had. She kicked herself for not knowing which way to go.

Maybe it was time to yell for Robbie and Thatch – yet what good would it do if they found her? Then all of them would be lost.

"Are you thinking what I'm thinking?" Jeff asked in a quiet voice.

"We overshot the path?" TJ answered. "Or it veered one way and we veered the other?" He slumped on to a rock. "Trail markers."

"Huh?"

"We should have used our trail markers when we left the path. Aunt Jenny put some in both backpacks in case we got separated."

TJ reached into a side pocket and drew out a handful of red plastic flagging.

"I didn't think we were going that far." Jeff's voice rose in defence. "I didn't think we *needed* to mark the way."

"Wrong," TJ said, correcting him. "You didn't think at all. You *forgot* the trail markers."

"Well, so did you."

He ignored Jeff's comment, which, Beka assumed, meant it was true.

Instead, he said, "Let's use our brains."

"Ha – it's about time." Beka chuckled even though she was as guilty as they were.

TJ gestured at the overgrown hillside. "This is certainly no place to set up camp. We need to find a level spot."

"The ground was flat on the other side of the stream."

"Are you sure?"

"Yeah. All we have to do is head back towards the tall pine." Jeff twirled, searching for the tree. "There it is, see? We cross the stream, and find a flat spot – not too near the water – to please Aunt Jenny."

"Are you positive it's the same pine tree?"

"Look at all the birds."

"Yeah, like that's the only tree birds flutter around." Without waiting for a response, TJ adjusted his pack and got ready to move. "I guess your plan's as good as any."

Beka wasn't thrilled about traipsing through the undergrowth again, but she had no choice. She only hoped Robbie would be able to find her before dark. Maybe ghosts in storybooks were supposed to *like* the dark of night, but she didn't. Never had; never would.

They returned to the bank of the river. Jeff hopped on to a few stones, kneeling to feel the water. "It's cold," he called over the noisy torrent.

"Of course it's cold. It's a mountain stream." TJ gazed towards heaven and shook his head.

Beka remembered Aunt Jenny making the same gesture last night when Jeff asked what time breakfast would be served this morning.

"How are we supposed to get across the water?" TJ hollered. "Swim?"

Jeff hopped back to the bank and headed upstream.

"No!" Beka shouted. "You're on an *island*. Go *down*stream, towards the shore. Not deeper into the forest."

TJ followed without question.

"You're both going the wrong way," Beka called. "How come *I* know this and you don't? I don't even *have* an Aunt Jenny."

Fifteen minutes later, Beka mentally apologized to Jeff. He *had* found a way across. A fallen log lay half in, half out of the water. It allowed them to get close enough to the far bank to jump to the other side.

Beka watched the cousins awkwardly inching their way along the slippery log, hanging on to each other.

"Watch this!" Stepping into the icy stream, Beka waded across. She slipped on the rocks, and lost her balance a few times because of the swift current. And at one point the water came clear up to her waist. But when she climbed on to the far bank, she was as dry as when she started.

Being a ghost had its advantages.

Leaning against an aspen tree, Beka waited for the cousins.

TJ made a smooth jump, landing on his hands and knees in a gooseberry patch.

Jeff wobbled, lost his balance, and landed with one foot in the stream. When he yanked his hand from his pocket to steady himself, his hat and one glove went flying.

They watched the hat and glove float swiftly away.

Jeff pulled himself on to the bank. One leg was soaked from the thigh down. "Let's go," he called, acting as if he'd meant to dip one leg into the icy stream.

Fifty yards beyond the bank, they found a grassy area, flat and free of rocks, as Aunt Jenny had ordered. "This is it," Jeff said, dumping his backpack on to the ground. "Home sweet home."

"Well." TJ took stock of their surroundings. "This will do, I guess." He dumped his pack next to Jeff's. "Now we'll have to hustle to round up enough firewood before it gets dark." Groaning, he stretched his sore muscles. "Surviving is tough work."

Beka lagged behind, near the stream. Too much time had passed since her brother had left to find Thatch. "Robbie!" she shouted. "Thatch! Can you hear me?"

She glanced at the dense surroundings. Already the late afternoon sun had dipped below the tallest treetops. How would her brother ever find her this far from the path? Would he guess the group had crossed the stream?

Beka frowned at the darkening sky. "HURRY, RAZ!" she yelled. "PLEASE FIND US!" To herself she whispered, "You *promised* you'd come when I called."

Standing still, she listened for an answering shout from her brother, or an anxious bark from Thatch. But the only replies that met her ears were vague rustlings from the afternoon forest.

Chapter 12
Lost and Found

Beka perched on a rock while the cousins rolled sleeping-bags on to inflated mats to cushion the hard ground.

Jeff scouted the area for rocks, piling them in a circle to enclose the evening's fire. TJ gathered wood and tinder, making frequent trips to stack his armload next to the fire circle.

As daylight dimmed into twilight, they moved faster and faster. Beka was impressed. The boys *did* seem to know a thing or two about setting up camp – thanks to their aunt.

Mixed emotions played tag inside her mind. Robbie had been gone for *hours*. Had something happened? Couldn't he find her? Or was he still searching for Thatch?

She hoped it wasn't the latter. The thought of losing good ol' Thatch made her feel like crying.

Impatient, she hopped off the rock to pace. Why hadn't she gone with her brother instead of staying with the boys? She hadn't been a whole lot of help to them. They'd managed to lose their way in spite of her.

Now they seemed fine. They didn't need her hovering around.

Robbie should have stayed while *she* went after Thatch. After all, he was the one who wanted to "go camping" in the first place. He'd be having a great time now. She, however, was bored.

Jeff built his fire circle until the rocks were almost as high as his knees. TJ arranged the twigs and tinder (the way Aunt Jenny had taught him), then lit the fire. Flames leaped high, crackling and hissing, filling the area with the pleasant scent of wood smoke.

Twilight dipped into evening without much warning. The boys pulled extra clothing from their packs. Jeff never mentioned his missing hat, or why he wore a single glove. One glare stifled TJ's snickering.

"Raz!"

Beka had just started to take a seat on another rock. Startled, she misjudged the seat, and landed with a thud on the ground.

Robbie grinned down at her, his face pale and almost see-through in the flickering firelight.

A second later, Thatch was all over her, licking and nuzzling as if *she'd* been lost instead of him.

"Don't scare me like that." Beka tried to sound irritated, but she was so relieved to see them, she couldn't hide her smile. "What took you so long?" she asked, climbing back on to the rock.

Thatch was off to investigate the cousins. They were taking stock of the remaining food and arguing over what to eat now and what to save for later.

The distracted look in Robbie's eyes told Beka he'd rather help the boys set up camp than answer her questions. As a boy scout, he was always building wigwams and lean-tos and snow houses.

"Hello?" Beka tapped his shoulder to remind him she was still waiting for an answer.

"Well, first, I couldn't find Thatch, but I *did* find tons of squirrels. You know how much he loves chasing them. So all I could do was keep looking."

Pausing, he climbed on to the rock next to her. "I tracked Thatch all the way to the east shore. A group of teenagers were having a picnic, and he was right in the middle – playing volleyball and chasing this plate-shaped thing the kids sailed through the air at each other. I had a hard time convincing Thatch to leave.

"Then I told him to find you. That worked. And he did a great job of tracking you until we got part way up the path. Then he took off down the side of a hill."

Robbie stopped to listen to the boys discuss whether or not they needed to build a wickiup. (No, they decided. Too tired.)

Beka could tell Robbie was disappointed.

Especially since he knew what a wickiup was. "Go on with your story," she urged.

He clicked his fingers to call the dog away from the fire. "Keeping up with Thatch was hard; I'm glad he has white fur. Once we got to the stream, he lost your scent. I guessed you'd crossed over, so we did, too. Then it took a while for Thatch to pick up the scent again and find you."

The twins watched the boys attempt to rig a pan holder over the fire with a Y-shaped stick on each side and a straight stick across the top. Their effort kept tumbling down. Finally, TJ hooked the pan on to the end of a stick and held it over the fire like a fishing rod.

"They're not doing it right," Robbie groaned. "*I* know how to make it work." He started to get up, then stopped, realizing he couldn't help them.

"This is too much trouble for one cup of hot chocolate," TJ mumbled. "Next time, we're bringing a microwave."

"Only if you carry it," Jeff teased, filling

mugs with powdered chocolate.

"Mmmm," Robbie moaned. "Remember hot chocolate?"

The boys made peanut butter and raisin sandwiches. Thanks to Jeff, there were no biscuits for dessert, or marshmallows to roast over glowing embers.

Night brought a quick dip in temperature. The cousins pulled their sleeping-bags close to the fire. Jeff balanced his one wet hiking boot on the hot rocks to dry it out. TJ chose two fat logs to get the flames roaring again before they climbed into their bags.

Thatch circled the fire a few times, then made himself comfortable on top of Jeff's sleeping-bag – meaning on top of Jeff.

"We might as well get comfortable, too." Robbie stood, looking for a better spot to spend the night.

"I hate it here," Beka mumbled. "Can't we take the canoe and go home? I went to all that trouble to get the guys out of my attic. Now I can't enjoy it."

She tried to ignore the disagreement in her

brother's eyes. "Why should *we* spend an uncomfortable night here?" she asked. "We can come back in the morning before they wake up."

"But what if something happens, and they need to get back to the mainland? They'd be stranded here without a canoe."

Robbie dropped to one knee, as if he were prepared to beg. "Are you really bored?"

"Yes." She left off the part about feeling scared and being afraid of the dark, too — dumb traits for a ghost.

"Then will you stay if I promise to entertain you? Please?"

Beka gave in. Curiosity over how Robbie planned to entertain her got the better of her. "OK," she said finally. "Be my ghost."

Chapter 13
How to Haunt a Campsite

Robbie wandered between the sleeping-bags and fire, head bowed, planning for the evening.

On the outskirts of the area, he stooped to take hold of a rock, focusing on it until it moved in his hand – meaning it disappeared from sight and moved into his dimension. Soon he'd collected a pile of rocks in his shirt-tail.

Tossing the first one into the air, he and Beka watched it land in a bed of crinkly leaves around the base of a blackjack oak.

Whoooosh!

The rock sparked white as it became visible again.

Jeff shot upright, making Thatch spring to his feet, barking. "W-what was that?"

"Probably an animal," came TJ's muffled reply.

"How are we going to protect ourselves?" Jeff's voice wavered. "Maybe we *should* build a wickiup."

"We've got a fire. Animals won't go near a fire."

"Who says?"

"Aunt Jenny."

"What if the fire dies in the middle of the night?"

"The animals will eat you."

"TJ!"

TJ sat up, grinning. "We'll keep the fire burning all night. No big deal."

Jeff looked relieved. "I'm not ready to sleep yet."

"I thought you were tired from staying awake in the attic all night."

"I didn't say I wasn't tired. I said I'm not ready to sleep."

"Fine. Me neither."

"Let's eat again."

TJ tossed a handful of sand in his direction. "We're almost out of food, cuz. You're not eating *my* breakfast tonight."

"Then let's tell stories."

TJ laughed. "You'll get too scared. You wouldn't even turn off the light in the attic last night."

"I won't get scared." He flung a handful of sand back at his cousin.

"All right." TJ brushed sand off his sleeping-bag. "You tell the first story."

Jeff leaned back on his elbows, thinking.

Robbie circled the area, tossing another rock near the boys.

Plunk!

Jeff sucked in his breath. Even TJ stopped to listen.

Jeff's gaze darted from one dark shadow to the next as he began his story in a shaky voice. "Have you heard the one about the guy who has a hook instead of a hand? He—"

"A million times, Jeffrey. *Everyone's* heard that story a million times."

Plink! A rock hit the boulder Beka was sitting on.

"Hey, you did that on purpose," she teased.

"Are you enjoying my show?" Robbie called. "I call it *How to Haunt a Campsite*."

"It's better than a Barnum and Bailey circus."

Robbie dumped the rest of the rocks into the fire.

Jeff's eyes bugged out as sparks from the rocks mingled with flames. "If you don't like my story," he said in a quiet voice, "then *you* tell one."

TJ grinned. He pulled his knees up, sleeping-bag and all, and settled in comfortably. "Once upon a time, there was a pudgy little kid who travelled to a distant island, searching for a magic pond. One night—"

"Stop it."

"Why?"

"You're making fun of me."

"Me? Make fun of you? Nev—"

Suddenly a scream split the air, followed by a loud crack and a swooshing noise. Both boys scrambled from the sleeping-bags and fumbled in the dark for their jackets.

Chills raced up Beka's spine. "Good job, Rob. You scared *me* that time."

The cousins stood frozen, panting hard, backed so close against the fire Beka was afraid their clothes might scorch.

Robbie touched her shoulder.

Flinching, she twirled to face him. "How'd you get behind me? I thought you were over there." She flung her arm in the direction of the noise.

Before he could answer, she continued, "I think it's time to stop making spooky noises. I'm starting to feel sorry for these guys."

Robbie's face looked as pale as the boys'.

"Rob, what's wrong?"

"I didn't make those noises," he stammered. "I – I thought you did, while I was circling around behind you."

Then Beka noticed Thatch's fur. Standing on end. A growl in his throat erupted into a suspicious howl, unlike anything she'd ever heard.

Before she could leap from the rock and grab his collar, he bolted into the darkness.

"Let's go home," Jeff blurted.

TJ started to speak, but his voice wasn't there. He cleared his throat. "We can't go home. Aunt Jenny would never forgive us." He took a brave step in the direction of the mysterious noises, then stopped. "It was probably a raccoon."

"Raccoons don't make noises like that," Robbie said.

"Raccoons don't make noises like that," Jeff echoed. Backing up one more step, he knocked his boot into the fire.

After much yelling and screaming, TJ fished Jeff's boot from the flames with a thick stick. The laces had burned completely and the glue holding the rubber sole had melted, making it fall away. The putrid smell of burning rubber polluted the air.

"Ugh," TJ said, tossing the smoking boot into the dirt.

With a defeated sigh, Jeff slumped on to his sleeping-bag.

Beka ignored the cousins' latest disaster. She was too worried about Thatch to wonder how Jeff was going to hike out of there with only one boot.

Should *she* go after Thatch this time? Would he be OK against whatever was out there in the midnight forest?

Beka's memory kept reminding her that Mystery Island had never brought them anything but bad luck.

Chapter 14
Act Like Ghosts

"Why don't we go together this time?" Robbie tried to sound casual, but Beka could tell by his voice the unexpected noises had unnerved him, too.

"You mean, go together to look for Thatch?"

"Yep."

"I was afraid that's what you meant," Beka squirmed, feeling uncomfortable. She'd rather stay put, close to the fire. "Can't we just *call* him back?"

Robbie's look reminded her Thatch had a mind of his own. "Sis, there's no reason to be scared. We're ghosts, remember? Nothing can harm us."

"Oh, yeah? How about *other* ghosts?"

"Mmmm. Hadn't thought of that." He shoved hair from his eyes the way he did when something made him nervous. "Thanks for bringing it up."

"I'm going to find a hefty stick," TJ said, stepping out of the circle of light while fumbling to turn on a torch.

Jeff stayed by the fire. Having only one boot might've had something to do with it. He couldn't find a good stick, so he picked up a rock and studied it. "Like *this* is going to scare off whatever made that horrible noise," he mumbled.

More noises echoed from the darkness. "Hey!" came an irritated voice.

Jeff twirled. "TJ? Is that you?"

"Who else?" he snarled. "Get over here!"

Jeff took three baby steps and stopped. "Are you alone?"

"No. The axe murderer of Mystery Island is holding me hostage."

"Stop it," Jeff said. "Turn on the torch so I can see you."

"It *is* on. The batteries are dying. Why didn't you change them?"

Jeff hopped on one boot toward TJ's shouting.

The twins beat him there. They found TJ lying on the ground.

Jeff fell to his knees. "What happened?"

"I stepped into a hole and twisted my ankle," TJ said in a dull voice. "Something snapped like a pencil lead when I fell."

He shoved the useless torch at Jeff. "Look how puny this light is. Number three on Aunt Jenny's list under *Before You Leave* says 'Always put fresh batteries into your torch.'"

Jeff shook it and clicked it on and off, but the light didn't grow any brighter. "At least I *brought* a torch. Why didn't *you* bring one?"

"Because you said we could share yours." TJ tried to get up, then sank to the ground again. "I've probably broken my ankle. You're gonna have to be a hero, and save me."

"A hero?" Jeff repeated, as if the idea greatly appealed to him.

He hoisted TJ on to his good leg. They hobbled back to the light. Jeff dumped TJ on top of his sleeping-bag – a bit too hard.

"Thanks a lot," TJ snapped. "Here's your stupid torch. Go see what made that noise."

The instant he said it, a faint moaning sound filled the night air.

If the cousins' faces grew any whiter, Beka thought, it would be hard to tell which two were the ghosts.

"They'll be fine," Robbie said. "Let's go and find Thatch."

"Will *we* be fine?" Beka mumbled, but she followed.

They headed in the direction of the original noises, and found a rocky ridge. Shrubs pushed the twins towards the uneven edge as they moved. Pebbles and pinecones scattered along the ridge made them slip.

"I think an animal must have lost its footing along here and slid down the ravine," Robbie said.

Beka wished *they* had a torch. Or that the moon would come out from behind the clouds so they could see. "I don't—"

Before she could finish, her feet skidded on the gravel, flipping her over the edge. Slipping and sliding for what seemed like minutes, she splashed into water at the bottom.

"Are you OK?" Robbie yelled.

Beka lay on her back and tried to make out the pointy treetops against a muted sky. "I think I'm dead," she yelled back.

"Don't be redundant," he called, sounding relieved.

Beka groaned.

"Don't move," Robbie commanded. "I'm on my way down. On my feet, I hope."

"I'm not going anywhere." She moved her arms and legs to make sure they still worked. Suddenly a familiar whine met her ears. "Puppy?" she whispered. "Are you here?" Thatch sniffed at her, then nudged her rib cage as if he wanted her to move.

"I found Thatch!" she called, knowing Robbie would be pleased. As she reached to pet him, a strange feeling swept through her. It was the same one she had whenever she was taking up the same space as another person.

Another person? Here?

"Yikes!" Beka cried, scrambling to her feet.

"What's wrong?" Robbie shouted. "I'm coming as fast as I can."

Although the overcast sky kept the stars or moon from offering much light, Beka could make out the figure of a person lying half in and half out of the water. Faint, ragged breathing told her the person was still alive.

"Who *is* this?" she whispered to Thatch.

Thatch whined again, standing guard over the victim.

Robbie arrived, accidentally splashing into the water. "I didn't know the stream curved around this way," he said. Then, "Hey, there's a person here!"

"No kidding. I don't know who it is. It's too dark to make out their features."

"What are we going to do?" Robbie's concern matched hers. "Whoever it is needs help. It's cold out here. And they've gotten wet."

"The boys will have to do the saving," Beka said. "Or at least Jeff will. I don't think TJ is going to be any help at all."

"How are we going to get Jeff down here?"

Beka glanced up the hill where the boys were camped. She thought about last night in the attic, and how she'd carved a circle around Jeff, giving him *hints* until her words broke into his consciousness.

"I know a way," she replied. "All we have to do is go up there and act like ghosts."

Chapter 15
Help is on the Way ... I Hope

Climbing the ravine took a lot longer than sliding down on her bottom, Beka noticed.

At the campsite, TJ lay on top of his sleeping-bag, moaning in pain while Jeff thumbed through his *First-Aid Pocket Guide*.

"Do something," TJ hissed, cradling his sore ankle in his arms. "Fast."

Robbie tried to read the first-aid guide over Jeff's shoulder. "How are we going to convince him to climb down the ravine if TJ keeps him here?"

Beka had already begun to circle the area. Since she'd managed to distract Jeff while he was playing Cluedo, surely she could now.

"Hurry up," TJ whined. "What does the booklet say?"

Jeff cleared his throat and began to read. "First, check to see if the victim is breathing."

"I'm breathing," he snapped. "Skip ahead to broken ankles."

Jeff leafed through the pages, angling them towards the fire so he could read. "Does it hurt?"

"Of course it hurts. And *you're* going to hurt, too, if you don't speed it up."

"I'm *trying*. It's hard to read in the dark." Riffling through the booklet, he squinted at the words in the firelight.

Beka tightened her circle. Each time she passed close to Jeff, she chanted. "*Follow me.*" Or "*Someone needs you.*" Or, "*It's urgent.*"

Jeff began to act distractedly. "The book says if your ankle is broken, it's best to leave your boot on because it holds the bones in place."

"Fine. I can do that. Then what?"

Jeff lifted his head, listening.

"*Stop what you're doing,*" Beka told him.

"Follow me. Down the hill. Now!"

"Jeff-rey!" TJ growled.

He flinched, squinting at the words again. "Next it says *seek medical help*."

"Great." TJ fell back on to his sleeping-bag. "So what are you waiting for? Go seek medical help."

"Now?"

He was quiet for a moment. "Guess not. There isn't much we can do until morning. You'll have to help me make it to the canoe."

Jeff didn't answer. He was too busy listening to a voice in the wind.

"Cuz?"

Rising slowly to his feet, Jeff's gaze almost followed Beka's circle.

"What's wrong?" TJ stopped to listen.

"I-I don't know." Jeff moved towards the rocky ridge as though he were in a trance.

"Yes!" Beka hurried ahead of him. "That's what I want you to do. Come on." Turning, she led the way.

"Good job," Robbie told her. "It's working."

"Hey, where are you going?" In the reflection of the fire, TJ's eyes widened. "You don't have to go for help now. Please. Don't leave me here alone."

Jeff smirked, as if it amused him to see his cousin weak and begging. "I'm not leaving. I just have to go and look at something over there." He pointed into the darkness. "Give me your left boot."

"Why?"

"I can't traipse off into the forest with one shoe and one sock."

With great reluctance, TJ pulled the boot off his uninjured leg and handed it over. Jeff put it on, then reached for the torch. The dim light wavered, as if it couldn't make up its mind whether or not to shine.

"See?" TJ said. "The light isn't strong enough to reach the ground. That's why I didn't see the hole that swallowed my foot."

Jeff tried to use it anyway, tiptoeing cautiously away from camp.

"Where are—?"

"I'll be right back!" he hollered at TJ. "Stay there."

"Right. Like I'm planning on going any-where."

"This way," Beka coaxed, finding an easier way down the ravine than the route she had taken earlier.

Jeff stepped on to the ridge. He looped the torch around the trees and the drop-off. Didn't help. Seeing anything beyond a few inches was impossible. Clicking off the light, he shoved it into his pocket.

"After you," Robbie said, gesturing for Jeff to start down the hill.

The boy seemed confused, as if he really didn't think this was a good idea. Turning abruptly, he headed back toward the circle of light.

"No!" Robbie threw both hands in the air, as if to block his way. "Go *down* the hill," he cried. "*Down. Down. Down.*"

Jeff stopped.

"That's it," Beka yelled. "Keep talking to him."

She stationed herself at the bottom of the ravine. "Come *here*, Jeff! Hurry! Someone needs your help."

He shrugged. "This is stupid," he said to no one in particular.

A few steps later, he slipped off the ridge, sliding half-way down before he could stop. Mumbling under his breath, he came to his feet, dusted himself off, then stumbled the rest of the way.

Thatch barked a few times, as if he wasn't sure if the dark form approaching him was coming to hurt or help the victim he guarded.

"It's OK, puppy. Help is on the way," Beka cooed, patting Thatch's head. "At least I hope it is."

Jeff tiptoed around the area. He acted as if he were looking for something he'd lost, but couldn't remember what it was.

Robbie attempted to stay on Jeff's heels. "To your left," he shouted. "Go *left* five steps. Stop! Turn right. Walk straight."

Beka was amazed to see Jeff do exactly what Robbie told him – although not in a timely manner. "He's going too far to the right," she warned, wishing she could grab his sleeve and jerk him to where she wanted him.

"If he doesn't stop, he'll walk right into the—"

Splash!

"Stream," Beka finished.

"Rats!" Jeff cried. "The stream. Why didn't I hear it?"

He swiped at his soaked leg a few times. "At least *both* of my legs are wet now instead of only one."

"And you're down to one dry boot between the two of you," Robbie said, joining them.

As Jeff straightened, his hand brushed against the victim, making the person moan softly.

Jeff jumped so far, he landed back in the water. Fumbling for the torch, he clicked it on. "Who's there?" His voice was a hoarse whisper.

What he saw in the faint light told him the person needed help. Sloshing out of the water, he fell to his knees. Gingerly he touched one arm, then turned the light towards the person's face.

Beka gasped. So did Robbie and Jeff. In one faint voice they cried, "Aunt Jenny!"

Chapter 16
Ghosts Don't Get Any Respect

Jeff stayed frozen in one position for so long, Beka began to wonder what was wrong with him. She expected him to fall over in a dead faint. Then the twins would have *two* people to rescue.

"Aunt Jenny," he finally whispered. "What are you doing here? Are you hurt?"

His only answer came from an owl somewhere in the darkness.

"It's all up to me," he said in a shaky whisper. "TJ's up there with a broken ankle and you're down here…" His voice trailed off since he didn't know *why* she was down here or what was wrong with her. "I wish I knew what to do. I *wish* I could be a hero for once in my life."

"Help," he whispered to the night, then pulled out the first-aid booklet. The pitiful glow from the torch barely lit the page. "I should know all this stuff by now; we talk about it in Scouts all the time."

He stayed silent for a moment, reading. "Yes," he finally said. "The *ABC*s. I need to check the *ABC*s."

"What does *that* mean?" Beka nudged Robbie with her elbow to make sure he was still close by. Thatch she could see, thanks to his bright fur.

"Don't know," her brother said.

"*A*," Jeff began. "What does *A* stand for?"

"Beats me," Beka answered.

"That starts with a *B*," Robbie said.

"Air!" Jeff exclaimed. "Please be OK, Aunt Jenny. Please be getting enough air." He loosened the collar of her shirt.

"*B*. *B* is breathing." He leaned close to her, listening. The faint sound of breathing was his answer. "Good," he said, his voice filled with relief.

"*C. C* stands for pulse."

"Huh?" Beka said. "This guy doesn't know how to spell."

"*C* stands for circulation," Robbie said. "It's coming back to me now."

When Jeff placed his fingers alongside Aunt Jenny's neck to check her pulse, she shuddered, catching her breath with a sharp hissing sound.

"What...?" She winced, as if it hurt to speak. Startled, she tried to struggle into a sitting position. "Where...?" She sounded confused, like she was waking from a nightmare.

Aunt Jenny's panic upset Thatch. He began to bark.

"Stop moving!" Jeff commanded. "Lie still."

His aunt did as she was told. "Who...?"

"It's me. Jeff." He turned the light on to his face, but it only made him look like a phantom with black sockets where his eyes should have been.

Suddenly Aunt Jenny realized her right side lay in the water. She scooted over. "Ouch!" she cried. "Oh, great. I think my arm is injured. And my leg." She tried to wiggle each one, then stopped to groan. "Where's TJ?"

"He stayed at our campsite." Jeff motioned towards the top of the hill. "I came down here to see what was making all the noise."

Beka sniggered. "He's fudging. He never would have come down here if it hadn't been for us."

"Right," Robbie agreed. "Ghosts don't get any respect."

Hugging herself, Aunt Jenny began to shake from the cold night air.

"Do something, Jeff," Beka urged. "She's got the chills."

"Here's what you need to do." Aunt Jenny's voice was so weak, Beka could barely hear her.

"Hush," Jeff blurted. "Here's what *you* need to do. Lie still while I finish checking to make sure you're OK. I need to move you further from the stream and get you dry."

Aunt Jenny was speechless at her nephew's

orders. Her shivering became worse. She tried to wrap her arms around herself.

"I'll build you a fire, then drag my sleeping-bag down here for you. You're soaking wet; you'll freeze out here."

"Jeffrey, I'm so impressed—"

"Don't call me Jeffrey."

"Yes, sir."

"And another thing."

Aunt Jenny wiggled further from the water. "Yes?"

"What are you doing here in the first place? Why are you sneaking around in the middle of the night, scaring us to death?" As he talked, he removed his jacket and folded it around her like a blanket. Then he pulled off his sweater, rolled it up, and slipped it under her head for a pillow.

"Thank you," she whispered, avoiding his questions.

"Aunt Jenny." His voice was stern.

"OK, OK." She pulled his jacket tight, blocking the chilly wind. "I sent you boys over here alone, and I knew you'd *probably* be fine."

Beka noticed her emphasis on the word *probably*.

"But … you *are* my responsibility, and I promised your parents I'd take good care of you. I followed you over and camped nearby to keep an eye on you. That way, if you needed me, or if anything went wrong, I'd be right here."

"How did you find us?" he asked. "How did you know where to look?"

She gave him a sidelong glance. "I trek through the wilderness for a living, remember? My only mistake was shutting off my torch so you wouldn't know I was there. That's when I fell off the cliff – or whatever it was."

"Well, you didn't have to spy on us." He sounded defensive. "We're doing fine."

"Aren't you going to mention getting lost? Chasing after the magic pond? Falling into the stream, losing your hat and glove, eating most of the food? Burning up your boot and TJ's injury?" Beka shook a finger at him. "Doesn't sound fine to me."

Robbie chuckled. "Now's not the best time to bring all that up."

"I'm glad everything is going well," Aunt Jenny told him. "Still – if anything happened to one of you, and I wasn't here, your parents would never forgive me. *I'd* never forgive me."

She started to get up.

"Stay," Jeff commanded. "I'll go after my sleeping-bag and matches, then build you a fire, and—"

"Why don't you just help me up to your campsite?"

"Because my first-aid book says not to move the victim in case there are internal injuries."

"Oh. I guess I am *the victim*." She was quiet for a moment, as though evaluating her own injuries. "My leg may be broken. And my arm is injured. But inside, I'm OK. With your help, I can make it up the hill."

"Didn't you bring a sleeping-bag?" Jeff said.

"Sure I did. It's back at my camp, a quarter of a mile that way." She pointed towards the dark forest at the top of the ridge.

"Oh."

"Volunteering to go and get it is the last thing he wants to do," Beka said.

"Well," Jeff rubbed his arms to get warm. "If I had a decent torch, I'd go and get your supplies."

After a few seconds of zipping and rustling noises, Aunt Jenny said, "Take my torch."

Jeff took it without replying. Was he sorry he'd acted so bravely? "Try to stand," he said. "We'll take our time getting up the hill. Then, um, I'll go and fetch your things."

He helped her to her feet, then added, "Did you bring a lot of food?"

"Of course," she said. "Lots of raisins and peanut butter."

Beka caught Jeff's grimace in the glare of the torch.

Aunt Jenny leaned against her nephew, holding her injured leg off the ground. "Jeffrey – I mean, Jeff," she began in a quiet voice, "I'm proud of you for being such a hero and for taking care of me."

"A hero?" he repeated, shrugging in embarrassment.

"But, I'm curious. What made you come down here to investigate the noises after I fell? That was very, very brave of you."

Taking a step, he waited for her to hop ahead on one foot. "I guess your city nephew is a lot tougher than you thought he was."

"Yeah, right, tough guy." Beka brushed past Jeff and started up the hill. "It's not nice to fudge to your aunt."

Chapter 17
Which Magic?

Lying in a pile of leaves at the base of a sycamore with Thatch's rump for a pillow was almost comfortable. "Just like old times," Beka sighed.

"Not exactly," Robbie answered, gazing at an opening in the clouds that allowed a few stars to peek through.

Beka watched the fire smoke. It was dying in spite of the cousins' best intentions to keep it blazing. She couldn't decide who was snoring the loudest – Thatch or TJ. The latter had escaped into slumber only after a dose of aspirin from his aunt.

Jeff was sleeping soundly after playing hero

again by going off alone to retrieve Aunt Jenny's supplies.

His aunt lay in her own sleeping-bag, wet clothes spread out near the fire to dry, hanging off the ground on branches rigged up by Jeff (with *subtle* instructions from Robbie).

The first light of dawn sliced through the remaining clouds, casting a pleasant haziness around the campsite that had seemed so spooky in the dark of night.

Jeff, first one out of his sleeping-bag, refused breakfast, much to the surprise of everyone – including the twins. He was in a hurry to get to the canoe, then off to the ranger station on the mainland to bring back help.

"What's with Thatch this morning?" Beka asked. The dog was practically lying on top of the campfire.

"Don't you remember his favourite part of camping?" Robbie tossed a stick to see if he could persuade Thatch to play instead of haunting the pile of smouldering coals.

"Ah, I do remember. Bacon. We always fried bacon."

TJ was the next one up. He tried hopping on his good foot to gather more firewood, then gave up in pain, hobbling back to his sleeping-bag.

Aunt Jenny couldn't get up at all. Her planned breakfast of hot oatmeal and biscuits smeared with apricot jam was shelved in favour of something easier – peanut butter and raisins.

"If I live to be a hundred," TJ grumbled, "I'm never eating peanut butter and raisins again."

"Know what?" Aunt Jenny said.

TJ held his breath and crinkled his brow, anticipating another lecture from his aunt.

"*I'm* never eating them again either," she said, making a goofy face.

It was the first time Beka had seen TJ laugh wholeheartedly all weekend.

Soon, Jeff returned with a group of park rangers. Trained as paramedics, they quickly stabilized Aunt Jenny's arm and leg. Thatch was in the middle of it all, acting possessively towards Aunt Jenny, as if he was personally responsible for saving her.

And maybe he was, Beka thought. The only reason *she'd* found Aunt Jenny was because she was looking for Thatch.

Two rangers carried Aunt Jenny up the hill to the path on a stretcher. Two others tended to TJ, whose ankle they suspected was sprained, but not broken.

Jeff rolled up the sleeping-bags and readied the backpacks for the return trip. He seemed distracted this morning, in spite of all the compliments coming his way.

"Is today's hero ready to leave?" Ranger Parella asked after the others had started back towards the path.

Jeff seemed pleased at the easy way people tossed around the word *hero*. "Um…" His gaze travelled the campsite, making sure he'd packed everything. "I'd like to stay for a while – if it's OK. I was working on a … um … mystery, and I haven't solved it yet."

"Ah," Beka exclaimed. "He still wants to find One Wish Pond."

"A mystery," repeated Ranger Parella. "Very

good. Are you planning to be a detective when you grow up?"

Jeff shrugged, as if the idea had never crossed his mind. "Maybe," he said. "Or I might lead wilderness tours, like my aunt Jenny."

Ranger Parella hoisted the extra packs. "The last tour boat to stop at Mystery Island docks at four. Be on the pier by then, and you can hitch a ride back."

"Thanks." Jeff waved goodbye as the ranger started towards the path.

"Well?" Robbie stood and stretched. "Do you want to catch a ride back in the rangers' boat? Or stay and see if Jeff bungles again, and needs us to rescue him."

"Mmmm. Let's wait a few minutes," Beka said. "I'm curious."

Jeff wandered towards the rocky ridge, stopping to study the area. "Why?" he asked out loud. "Why was I drawn to this ledge last night?" Not finding an answer, he worked his way down the ravine, stepping carefully to stay on his feet.

The twins followed.

Thatch kept whining nervously, as if he expected Jeff to need saving any second.

The boy wandered around the site where he had found Aunt Jenny, shrugged, then started back up the hill. All of a sudden he froze, twirling to take in the scene once more.

Beka noticed it the same moment Jeff did.

"This *isn't* part of the stream we crossed." Excited, he stepped to the edge of the water. "This isn't a stream at all." A grin spread across his face. "This is a *pond*. Yes! I found it!"

"Do you really think…?" Beka began.

"Sis, there are *zillions* of ponds on Mystery Island. Don't be silly."

Jeff paced the shore like he was about to explode with excitement. Thatch attempted to nudge him away from the water's edge. Even *he* sensed the guy was accident-prone.

Hopping on to a sawn-off tree stump, Jeff closed his eyes. "I wish," he began in a booming voice. Then his eyes flew open and he stopped.

"Wait, I've *already* wished." His voice was so quiet, Beka almost missed his words. Jeff spun around, staring up the hill, remembering. "I *wished* to be a *hero*. And … and Aunt Jenny called me a hero. So did Ranger Parella."

Suddenly his face crinkled in confusion. "That's not magic – is it?" He argued with himself for a moment. "Magic *must* have made me come down here in the first place. I *never* would have done it on my own; I was too scared to leave the fire. Something drew me here. The *pond* drew me here."

"Hey, don't *we* get any credit?" Beka sniffed.

"The pond," he repeated, staring at the water. "The pond granted me one wish. Just like the legend said it would. Wow, it *is* magic."

"Which magic?" Beka said. "Wishing magic or ghost magic?"

Satisfied, Jeff raced up the hill, hustling towards the path to catch up with the others.

"Guess he believes he found One Wish Pond after all," Robbie said.

"Well?" Beka tossed a pebble into the clear water. "Do *you* think it is?"

"Naw," Robbie scoffed. "Who believes in magic ponds?"

"Let's test it. Thatch! Come here."

The dog, who'd followed Jeff half-way up the hill, galloped down to Beka. Sitting on the shore, she took hold of his collar, and motioned for Robbie to sit beside her.

"I wish," she said, "to be home in my own quiet attic, peaceful and alone. Just me and Robbie and Thatch."

"Good wish," Robbie said. "Let's go and make it come true." He reached for Beka's hand to help her up.

As she took his hand, a foggy mist appeared from nowhere (from the pond?). Like a swirling shawl, it wrapped itself around the three of them, heavy and damp.

Beka gasped, closing her eyes against the eerie sensation of moist air lifting her, hurling her into a cloud. She grasped Robbie's hand and Thatch's collar with all her strength.

Suddenly the air cleared and the cloud

lifted. The three of them were sitting the same way as before, only they were sitting on the braided rug next to the bunk beds in the attic.

"Wow!" was all Robbie could say.

Beka couldn't say anything.

Thatch yawned, as if he, alone, understood what had just happened. In a mighty leap, he sprang on to the top bunk, settling down for a noonday nap.

"Raz," Beka said, finding her voice. "What happened?"

"Um … you made a wish at One Wish Pond and it was granted?"

"That's absurd. There's no such thing as a magic pond."

"You used to think there were no such things as ghosts."

"Mmmm. Good point. You mean, *we* caused the magic to happen? Not One Wish Pond?"

"I give up," Robbie said. "Did we?"

"You know what this means?" Excited, Beka came to her knees. "It means I have another ghost rule to add to my list: rule number ten." She paused to word it correctly: "Be careful what we wish when we're all holding on to each other – because it might come true."

"Woof," Thatch agreed, as if *he'd* known *that* ghost rule all along.

Rules to be Ghosts by...

1. Ghosts can touch objects, but not people or animals. Our hands go right through them.
2. Ghosts can cause "a disturbance" around people to get their attention. Here are three ways: walk through them; yell and scream a lot; chant a message over and over.
3. Rules of the world don't apply to ghosts.
4. Thatch's ghost–dog powers are stronger than ours. He can do things we can't. Sometimes he even teaches us things we didn't know we could do.
5. Ghosts can't move through closed doors,

walls, or windows (but we can *smoosh* through if there is one tiny hole).

6. Ghosts don't need to eat, but they can if they want to.

7. Ghosts can listen in on other people's conversations.

8. Ghosts can move objects by concentrating on them until they move into the other dimension and become invisible. When we let go of the object, it .becomes visible again.

9. Ghosts don't need to sleep, but can rest by "floating". If our energy is drained (by too much haunting or *smooshing*) we must return to Kickingbird Lake to renew our strength.

10. Ghosts can move from one place to another by thinking hard about where we want to be, and wishing it. All three of us must be touching to make it work.

Don't Miss!
The Mystery on Walrus Mountain –
Ghost Twins 3

"Robbie!" came Beka's voice. "You've got to *smoosh* back."

She sounded scared. But not as scared as *he* was right now.

Twirling, Robbie turned Thatch towards the wide blue yonder. *"Think*, Thatch. *Home."*

"Hurry!" Beka's voice did the trick. Thatch began to whine.

"Keep talking!" Robbie shouted. "And Thatch will come to you."

"Puppy!" Beka called. "Come here, Thatch. I need you!"

Thatch began to tremble. At first Robbie thought the dog was scared. Then a gust of icy wind smacked Robbie's face, and Thatch was gone.

The dog had *smooshed* without him!

"Rob, it's your turn!" Beka yelped. "Get out of there!"

"I'm trying," Robbie mumbled. *Beka. Picture Beka's face.* He wished his sister would call him home the way she'd called Thatch.

"Robert Adam Zuffel!" she hollered, as if she'd read his mind – like twins sometimes do. "Come home! Thatch and I need you!"

Dizziness swooped over him. *It's working*, he thought, eagerly focusing on the cold blueness of the winter sky, pretending it was the bed with the navy-blue quilt in his old room.

Then he made a big mistake. He peeked around the boulder.